ADVENTURES at TABBY TOWERS

Raintree is an imprint of Capstone Global Library Limited, a company incorporated in England and Wales having its registered office at 264 Banbury Road, Oxford, OX2 7DY – Registered company number: 6695582

www.raintree.co.uk
myorders@raintree.co.uk

Text © Capstone Global Library Limited 2018
The moral rights of the proprietor have been asserted.

ed 2018

Printed and bound in China.

ISBN 978 1 474 74883 4
21 20 19 18 17
10 9 8 7 6 5 4 3 2 1

British Library Cataloguing in Publication Data
A full catalogue record for this book is available from the British Library.

Every effort has been made to contact copyright holders of material reproduced in this book. Any omissions will be rectified in subsequent printings if notice is given to the publisher.

Fishing Frankie

by Shelley Swanson Sateren
illustrated by Deborah Melmon

CONTENTS

ADVENTURES at TABBY TOWERS

IT'S TIME FOR YOUR ADVENTURE AT TABBY TOWERS!

At Tabby Towers, we give cats the royal treatment. We are a first-class cats-only hotel that promises a safe, fun stay for all guests.

Tabby Towers has many cat toys and games. We make personal play time for every guest. And we have a large indoor kitty playground that will satisfy every cat instinct, including climbing and hunting. Also, your kitty will never tire of watching our cow and chickens from the big playground window.

We are always just a short walk away from the cats. Tabby Towers is located in a large, sunny, heated room at the back of our farmhouse. Every cat has a private litter box and a private, three-level "apartment", complete with bed, toys and dishes. Of course, we will follow your feeding schedule too.

TABBY TOWERS
WHO'S WHO

KIT FELINUS

Kit Felinus (fee-LEE-nus) is a lifelong cat lover. She has worked for cat rescue and shelter operations much of her adult life. After seeing the great success of Hound Hotel — the dog hotel next door — she realized the need for a cat hotel in the area. So she started Tabby Towers. She now cares for cats all day long and couldn't be happier!

TOM FELINUS

Tom Felinus is certain that his wife, Kit, fell in love with him because of his last name, which means "cat-like". He is a retired builder. He built Tabby Towers' kitty apartments, cat trees and scratching posts. He built the playground equipment too, which will keep your kitty happy for hours.

TABITHA CATARINA FELINUS (TABBY CAT, FOR SHORT)

Tabby Cat is Kit and Tom's granddaughter and a true cat lover. In fact, the cat hotel is named after her! She helps at Tabby Towers in summer. The 8-year-old daughter of two vets, Tabby lives in the city and has her own cat. She's read almost as many books about cats as her grandma has! Tabby will give your kitty all the extra attention or playtime he or she may need.

Next time your family goes on holiday, bring your cat to Tabby Towers.

Your kitty is sure to have a purr-fect time!

CHAPTER 1
Straight from the jungle

I'm Tabitha Catarina — Tabby Cat, for short. I'm *crazy* about cats. I've loved them my whole life. L-O-V-E-D, loved them! I even own a beautiful Himalayan cat called Bootsie.

Last spring, my parents decided to let me spend the summer at my grandparents' farm. Being with Grandma Kit and Grandpa Tom is great. But here's the best part: They run a cat hotel on their farm! It's called Tabby Towers.

I get to play with all kinds of cats and kittens seven days a week.

I truly am the luckiest girl alive.

There's only one problem. A big one. And her name is Alfreeda Wolfe.

Alfreeda is a girl my age who lives on the farm next door to my grandparents' place. She wants to be good friends with me, but some days that seems impossible. Here's why: She's *crazy* about dogs. That's fine, except she brags about them. She always puts down cats too. It makes me *so* cross.

Sometimes Alfreeda says things about cats that are total lies. Last month, she said some stuff that was completely wrong about a cat called Frankie. (Frankie was a guest at Tabby Towers then.) Alfreeda made my hair stand on end, just like the fur on an angry cat. I wanted to yell at her, "*Please* stop talking about cats!

You don't know anything about them! And it's really, really annoying!"

Maybe you're wondering if I really *did* yell at Alfreeda. Well, here's the whole story.

❧ ❧ ❧

It was early in the morning, in the middle of July. I had set my alarm extra early, because I couldn't wait to meet a new guest. A Bengal cat called Frankie had arrived at Tabby Towers late the night before. (I'd already gone to bed.) I knew a lot about Bengal cats, but I'd never seen one in real life.

I sprang out of bed and pulled on my leopard-print leggings. I put on a clean Tabby Towers T-shirt and my cat-eye glasses. Then I brushed my hair and pulled it up into a high ponytail. I always wear it sticking up high, the way a happy cat holds its tail.

I hurried down the corridor, tiptoeing past my grandparents' bedroom. Grandma Kit is an early riser, like me. But Grandpa Tom always sleeps until about lunchtime. That's because he's nocturnal, like cats. You see, cats hunt by instinct at night. So Grandpa Tom always stays up very late with the hotel guests. He plays all sorts of predator-prey games with them. He makes them feel like they're hunting or fishing in the wild.

I flew down the steps, hurried through the living room and leaped into the big farmhouse kitchen. Our neighbour Winifred Wolfe stood at the sink. She runs a dog hotel next door to us. She's a good friend of Grandma Kit's. She's also Alfreeda's mother. Yes, *that* Alfreeda – the girl who won't be quiet about how *great* dogs are, and how great cats *aren't*. Mrs Wolfe was busy washing Grandma Kit's hair.

"Good morning," I said.

"Hi, Tabitha!" Grandma Kit said, her head in the sink. Her voice sounded like it came from the bottom of a well.

"Good morning, Tabby Cat," Mrs Wolfe said in her usual cheerful voice. "We thought we'd cut your grandma's hair early, before our busy day begins."

Alfreeda's mum is the top dog groomer in the county. She's won lots of awards. She's great at cutting people's hair too.

"Grandma Kit, is Frankie here?" I asked. "Can I play with him? Is it safe to open the hotel door?"

Grandma Kit laughed. "Yes, yes and yes," she said. "The kitties are all safe in their apartments. Go ahead."

I hurried through a door next to the refrigerator. It led to the back of the house.

That's where Tabby Towers was. Grandpa Tom and Grandma Kit had turned their big family room into the cat hotel.

I rushed past the kitty playground to the row of kitty apartments. Each apartment was a small, three-level home with a screen door.

"Hi, you cute things," I said to kittens Fifi and Furbaby. They were a brother and sister who shared an apartment.

I peeked inside the second apartment and said good morning to another guest — a Persian cat called Child. Then I saw Frankie in his apartment and gasped.

Frankie was, paws down, the most handsome cat I had ever seen. He had beautiful orange fur. His back and sides were covered with brown, leopard-like spots. He had brown, tiger-like stripes everywhere else.

I started to talk to him in a soft, quiet voice.
It's important that first meetings with cats go
slowly and peacefully. I left the screen door
closed too, to help him feel extra safe. I knew
better than to touch a new guest too soon.

"Wow, Frankie, you're *big* for a house cat," I whispered. "You look like a small wild cat, straight from the jungle. Your eyes . . . they're such a beautiful, bright green."

"Meow," he said.

"You're welcome," I said with a quiet laugh.

"Meow, meow, meow," he said.

I laughed again. "I read in one of my cat books that you Bengals like to talk a lot."

"Meow." He pawed the screen door.

"Do you want to come out to play?" I asked. "We have a super-fun indoor playground with lots of toys."

"Meow!"

I opened the screen door and picked him up. "Your fur is *so* soft," I said. "And it *glitters*. It looks like you're covered with gold dust!

And wow . . . how much do you *weigh*? You are a big boy, aren't you?"

I carried Frankie over to the playground. "Look," I said. "There are cat trees and scratching posts. Ropes and ladders to climb. A cool kitty highway by the ceiling that you can zoom around. See the kitty see-saw? And the kitty swing? You can watch all the birds you want out of the big window. You can watch the chickens in the farmyard too. Or watch Cheesecake the cow in the –"

Suddenly Frankie leaped out of my arms. He landed on the worktop where Grandma Kit fills dishes with cat food. Then he slid right into the sink! It was about a quarter full of water and dirty cat-food dishes.

"Oh no!" I cried.

CHAPTER 2
A great fishercat

I jumped to save Frankie from the wet, dirty mess. I didn't want him to hate his first day at Tabby Towers!

But Frankie didn't hate falling into the sink. He loved it! He had so much fun.

At first, he tiptoed in the water. It came up to his knees. Then he started to splash around, pawing at the dirty bowls over and over. He slapped a spoon around too.

"Oh yeah," I said. "Now I remember. You Bengal cats love water, don't you?"

"Meow," Frankie said.

"You're part Asian leopard," I said. "I've read about your cousins, those leopards. They're wild cats that like to swim. They're great at fishing too. I bet you're a great fishercat."

"Meow."

"I thought so," I said. "You're not much different from your great-great-great grandparents, are you? That's so cool."

Frankie kept swatting at the bowls and spoon as if they were fish. Then he raised a paw and turned on the tap. What a trick! More water poured into the sink.

"Okay, that's enough," I said, turning off the tap. "You've already splashed water onto the floor. Guess who has to clean it up?"

"Meow?"

"That's right," I said. "*Me.*" I grinned and tickled him under his chin. "But I don't mind. You keep on swimming and fishing. It's fun, isn't it?"

Then I remembered something else I'd read about Asian leopards. Fishing isn't the *only* reason they go into lakes and rivers. Asian leopards dip into the water to go to the bathroom too. The water hides the smell from predators.

"Uh-oh!" I said. "Grandma Kit wouldn't want you to do *that* in the sink, Frankie. Come here, big boy."

I grabbed a towel and picked him up. I put him on the worktop and started drying him off.

Someone knocked on the Tabby Towers door, the one that led to the kitchen.

"All clear?" a voice called.

It was Alfreeda.

I groaned. I was supposed to call "all clear" to let the person entering Tabby Towers know that cats weren't sitting near the door, ready to sneak out. Guests at Tabby Towers had to stay in the cat hotel at all times. Safety first!

I didn't answer.

The morning was going purr-fectly so far. I just knew Alfreeda would wreck it somehow.

The door opened a slither. "Hey, Tabby Cat," Alfreeda called. "I know you're in there. Your grandma told me. Are you acting catty today?"

I wanted to yell, "Go away! I want Frankie all to myself!" But Grandma Kit always expected me to be nice to Alfreeda, no matter what.

The door opened a little further.

I kept rubbing Frankie with the towel. I kept my mouth shut too.

The door opened even wider.

"Come on, Tabby Cat," Alfreeda begged. "Let's hang out. You can come over and play catch with the dogs and me. I know cats never do anything fun. They just sleep all day."

I opened my mouth to say, "That is *not* true." But before I could say one word, Frankie sprang off the worktop. He flew through the air and out the door. Right past Alfreeda's feet.

"Catch him!" I cried.

⇒CHAPTER 3⇐
Furry orange cannonball

Alfreeda jumped backwards and crashed into the refrigerator.

"What was *that?*" she shouted. "It looked like a furry orange cannonball!"

"It was Frankie, our new guest," I cried, running into the kitchen. "Where did he go?"

"That way." Alfreeda pointed at the small cat door that led to the farmyard.

"Oh no!" I said. "Why didn't you stop him?"

"Hey, don't blame me," Alfreeda said.

"The only cat allowed to go outside is Scruffy," I said, almost shouting now. Scruffy was Grandma Kit's indoor-outdoor cat. "*Why* did you open the hotel door?"

"Sorry," she said.

I pushed past her and yelled, "Grandma Kit!"

I dashed through the living room and out the front door. Mrs Wolfe was cutting Grandma Kit's hair in the sunshine. Mrs Wolfe saw me and stopped cutting.

"What's wrong?" she asked.

"Frankie!" I cried. "He ran into the kitchen and out Scruffy's door. He's *outside*!"

Grandma Kit jumped up and threw the towel off her shoulders. She put on her glasses and raced down the porch steps. "Oh my. Look everywhere, Tabitha. The barn, the chicken coop, the meadow . . . everywhere!"

"Okay!" I said.

"I'll stay here and watch the cats in the hotel," Mrs Wolfe offered.

The search was on.

Grandma Kit, Alfreeda and I looked everywhere. We called, "Here, Frankie! Come here, boy! Where *are* you, Frankie?"

We couldn't find him. I'd never seen Grandma Kit look so worried.

"That poor cat could get hit by a car or truck," she said in a shaky voice. "People drive so fast on these country roads. Or he might get in a fight with a farm dog. Or someone might find him and keep him. Bengals are such beautiful cats. They're worth a lot of money."

"I'm really sorry," Alfreeda said. "I opened the door before Tabby Cat called 'all clear'."

"Well, all that matters now is that we find Frankie," Grandma Kit said. "Where else can we look?"

"I know," I said. "He might be playing in water somewhere. He loves it."

"I'm sure he does," Grandma Kit said. "He's a Bengal."

"What?" Alfreeda said with a roll of her eyes. "Cats *hate* getting wet."

I didn't have time to explain. "The ditch!" I said, running towards the road.

Grandma Kit and Alfreeda ran after me.

Smelly green water covered the bottom of the ditch. Flies buzzed. Frogs jumped. There was no sign of Frankie.

I pointed to the metal drainpipe that ran under the road. "Maybe he's in there," I said.

"He would *not* go in there," Alfreeda said. "Cats stay away from water. And that water is really, really disgusting. Even a dog would keep away from it."

"Frankie *likes* water, okay?" I said. "He doesn't care what colour it is or how it smells. He might be in that pipe, hiding from us. I have to look."

"Be careful, Tabitha," Grandma Kit said.

I moved through the tall grass and weeds to the edge of the ditch. I kneeled down and looked into the dark pipe.

"Frankie?" I called. "Are you in there?"

Frogs answered, but not Frankie.

"Can you see him?" Alfreeda asked.

"No, it's too dark to see anything at this end," I said. "Maybe I'll be able to see better at the other end."

I stood up – but I stood up too quickly.
My shoe slipped. I swung my arms in circles,
trying not to fall.

It didn't help.

I twisted and flew, face-first, towards the
water. The stinky green water.

"Yiiih!" I yelled, closing my eyes.

CHAPTER 4

Stay calm, Tabby Cat

I landed in the ditch on my hands and knees. Water splashed against my face. Mud squished between my fingers.

"Tabitha!" Grandma Kit cried. "Don't get a *drop* of that water in your mouth. It could make you very sick!"

"I won't," I said. "Just. Get. Me. Out of here!"

"Stay calm, Tabby Cat," Alfreeda said.

Grandma Kit reached out her hand. "You'll be okay," she said. "Just take my hand."

I looked at her, but I couldn't see her very well. "Oh! My glasses!" I cried. "They fell into the water."

I slowly started moving my fingers over the muddy bottom of the ditch. I felt in front of me and to my side. I touched small rocks, shells and plants. I think I even touched a drink's can. My knees sank deeper into the mud. Bugs buzzed around my face and neck.

Then my fingers touched something hard and smooth. "Found them," I said.

I pulled my glasses out of the mud, swished them in the water a bit and stood up.

"Okay, Tabitha, now try taking my hand again," Grandma Kit said.

I couldn't reach. "Come closer," I said.

"I can't," she said. "I'll fall in too!"

I tried to climb up the bank. But my shoes kept slipping, and I kept sliding straight back into the water.

Alfreeda carefully walked to the edge of the ditch. She stood between me and Grandma Kit. "Take my hand, Tabby Cat," she said. "You hold my other one, Mrs Felinus. On the count of three, Tabby, your grandma and I are going to pull you out. One . . . two . . . three!"

It worked. But unfortunately I looked and smelled horrible.

"Thank you," I said. "That's the most disgusting thing that's ever happened to me."

"You're just like a cat – not a fan of getting wet," Alfreeda said.

"I *like* getting wet. If the water's clean, that is," I said. "But Frankie wouldn't care if it's dirty. I bet he's in the drainpipe."

"Wash off that mud and slime, Tabitha," Grandma Kit said. "Alfreeda and I will keep looking."

"I just want to peek in the other end of the pipe quickly," I said.

First Grandma Kit shook her head. Then she said, "Okay. This time, though, lie on your stomach, on the road, and look down into the pipe from the top. Alfreeda and I will hold your feet so you don't fall."

I did what Grandma Kit said. I carefully leaned over the edge of the road and looked into the dark pipe.

"Frankie?" I called. "Are you in there, boy? Say something!"

Still nothing. Just frogs.

"He's not in there," I said over my shoulder.

Alfreeda helped me up, and the three of us walked back to the farmyard. I needed a long, hot shower. But for now, I just washed myself off with the cold water from the garden hose. We had to find Frankie.

"Where else might Frankie go for a swim?" Grandma Kit asked.

"Cheesecake's water tub?" I said.

We hurried to the cow's large drinking tub.

"Not here either," I said.

Grandma Kit groaned. "This is not good, girls," she said. "Tabby Towers could be in big trouble. If we lose Frankie, no cat owner will want to use our hotel ever again. They won't think it's safe."

"Wait," I said, snapping my fingers. "Bengal cats love playing in water, *and* they love fishing."

"No way," Alfreeda said. "Cats don't like getting their paws wet. *At all.* And they'd *never* want to do anything really fun, like go swimming or fishing. Not like dogs."

I wanted to shout, "*Wrong!*" But I didn't. Instead I said, "The lake. Lake Dee-Oh-Gee. Cats have a strong sense of smell. I bet Frankie could smell the fish in it from here."

"Yes!" Grandma Kit clapped her hands. "C'mon, let's hurry, girls. We have to get to Lake Dee-Oh-Gee and find Frankie!"

⇒CHAPTER 5⇐
Fishing for a plan

I ran down a long, winding path through the meadow. Then I entered the dark, cool woods and raced down the path towards the lake. Alfreeda and Grandma Kit followed.

I leaped around trees, over rocks and around huge green plants. I looked over my shoulder. Grandma Kit must've tripped over a root. Alfreeda was helping her up.

When I reached the edge of the woods, I looked down the long shoreline of the lake. And there he was – FRANKIE!

The runaway cat stood in the lake, staring at something in the still water. The water came up to his belly.

I lay on the sand, in tall weeds, so I wouldn't scare him away. My nose filled with the horrible smell of dead fish. I pinched it shut and heard Alfreeda behind me, chattering. I looked over my shoulder and put my finger to my lips.

"Shhh," I whispered. "Frankie's here. Tiptoe. Lie down."

Alfreeda and Grandma Kit crept over and lay in the weedy sand beside me. They both wrinkled their noses.

"Ew, it stinks," Alfreeda said, pinching her nose with her fingers.

"Like a hot beach covered in long-dead fish," Grandma Kit whispered.

That's what it was, exactly. Several dead fish floated near the shore of Lake Dee-Oh-Gee. A few had washed onto the sand close to where the three of us lay.

"Where is he?" Alfreeda whispered.

I parted the weeds and pointed.

"Oh wow!" Alfreeda gasped. "It's a *wild cat*! There haven't been wild cats around here in a long time. Or is it a *leopard*? Maybe it escaped from the zoo! Take a picture with your phone, Mrs Felinus. That'd be awesome for the front page of the town newspaper."

"No, dear," Grandma Kit whispered. "That's not a full-blooded leopard. That's Frankie. He's a Bengal. Bengal cats are part leopard."

"Really?" Alfreeda looked surprised.

Grandma Kit and I nodded.

"Wow." Alfreeda whistled quietly. "Beautiful."

"He certainly is," Grandma Kit said. "His owners really love him too. We have to catch him. But how are we going to do that, without scaring him off? If he runs into the woods at the other side of the lake, we may never find him."

My heart raced. I had to come up with a plan to help Grandma Kit, Tabby Towers and Frankie.

I fished around in my brain for a plan. Frankie kept sticking his paw in the water.

Suddenly he slapped a little fish right out of the lake. It flew towards the beach and plopped in the sand. Frankie leaped after it. He pawed the fish and bit it once. But he didn't eat it. He must not have been hungry. I knew that hunger had nothing to do with a cat's instinct to hunt or fish. Eating and hunting instincts came from different parts of a cat's brain.

Frankie tiptoed back into the lake. He stood still again, staring into the water below his chin. Then he slapped out another fish, and it landed in the sand.

"A fishing cat?" Alfreeda whispered. "This is *crazy*. Frankie has to be part dog."

"No, he isn't!" I snapped. "He's part Asian leopard, okay? Asian leopards swim and fish in the wild. Frankie has those instincts too. All Bengal cats do."

"I don't believe it," Alfreeda whispered. Her voice sounded annoyingly squeaky, thanks to her plugged nose. "Everyone knows that cats hate water."

I frowned. I opened my mouth to say something mean, but Grandma Kit gave me "the look". It was the one she often shot in my direction when Alfreeda was around. The look meant: *Tabitha, be nice. We're neighbours.*

I shut my mouth. Still, the hair on top of my head stood on end.

How can I sneak up and grab Frankie from behind? I wondered. There wasn't a bush or tree on the beach. He would see me coming.

I plugged my nose tighter. The stink was making it hard to think.

Then I realized something. I didn't have to sneak up at all. "That's it," I whispered. "I know how we can catch Frankie."

CHAPTER 6
Baiting the big kitty

"What's the plan, Tabby Cat?" Alfreeda asked.

"I'll show you," I said.

I picked up one of the very smelly, very dead fish out of the weeds. I held it by the tips of my pointer finger and thumb.

"Yuck!" Alfreeda said.

"I'm going to bait Frankie the Fishercat with his favourite smell," I said.

I held the fish far in front of my face and tried not to breathe.

I started to crawl across the sand, on my stomach. I crept very slowly towards Frankie. Without making a sound, I moved a few centimetres at a time.

Then I noticed Alfreeda was following me. I almost groaned out loud.

She crawled across the sand behind me. She held a dead fish too, plugging her nose with her free hand.

"Stay back," I whispered. "You'll scare Frankie away."

"It's double the dead-fish stink," she whispered back. "He'll jump at us, trying to get the fish. Then I'll grab him."

I wanted to yell, "No! *I'm* going to save Frankie!" But I didn't dare yell.

I took a couple of deep, quiet breaths and tried hard to calm down. Grandma Kit began to crawl behind Alfreeda. She held a dead fish too.

Quiet as three cats prowling towards prey, we crossed the sand.

When I got close to the water, Frankie raised his head. He turned slowly. He stared at the fish hanging from my fingertips.

Suddenly he leaped at me.

I jumped up and threw the dead fish over my shoulder. I raised my arms and spread them wide, ready to catch the flying furball.

He flew straight at me, like an orange and brown rocket.

Just then, Alfreeda's hip bumped mine. I fell sideways and landed in the sand.

"Hey!" I yelled. "You did that on purpose!"

"*I'll* get Frankie," she said, dropping her dead fish. "I caused this problem. I'll fix it."

Alfreeda raised her arms high in the air to catch Frankie.

CHAPTER 7
Kicking cat legs

Frankie landed with a *thud* on Alfreeda's chest. It was like she'd been hit by a sack of potatoes. She lost her balance and fell backwards, onto the sand.

"Oomph!" Alfreeda said, trying to hold Frankie in her arms.

He meowed and wiggled and twisted, trying to break free.

"He's so strong and heavy!" Alfreeda cried. "I can't hold him. Help!"

I dropped to my knees and reached into the tangle of kicking cat legs. I slid my fingers under Frankie's collar and held on tight.

"I've got him," I said in a soft, quiet voice. "You can let go, Alfreeda."

"No, you can't hold him by yourself, Tabby Cat!" she shouted. "It's like trying to hug a mountain lion!"

"Shhh, you'll scare him," I said in my most gentle voice. "I've got his collar. I'll take him. It's okay. You can let go."

Alfreeda sighed. Finally, she let go.

Frankie snuggled right up to my chest. His little heart pounded against mine. Still, I kept my fingers locked around his collar.

"Good work, girls," Grandma Kit said. "Let's go home."

She led the way to Tabby Towers, holding a dead fish in front of Frankie and me. The smell was horrible but worth it. He didn't try to wiggle out of my arms at all.

☙ ☙ ☙

Five minutes later, we reached Tabby Towers.

"You found Frankie!" Mrs Wolfe cried. "That's great!"

"Yes," Grandma Kit said. "But now Frankie knows there's a lake nearby. I'm afraid he will try to escape again. We'll have to watch him every second when he's out of his apartment."

"Would it be helpful if Alfreeda stayed a while and watched him?" Mrs Wolfe asked Grandma Kit.

Oh no, I thought. *Even* more *time with Alfreeda? This day just keeps getting worse.*

I felt like telling the grown-ups, "Trust me, Alfreeda will *not* be useful around here. She will just cause more trouble." But I kept my mouth shut.

"That would be helpful, Winifred," Grandma Kit said. "Tabitha needs a shower and clean clothes. While she's upstairs, Alfreeda can watch Frankie. Thank you."

"Okay!" Alfreeda grinned. "I have to wash my hands first, though. They *stink*."

Mrs Wolfe promised to finish cutting Grandma Kit's hair that evening, then she left. I put Frankie on the kitty swing and gave him a gentle push. But he jumped right off. He ran straight to the door that led to the kitchen. He pawed the door, over and over, and cried really loudly.

"He wants to go back to the lake," I said.

"You're right," Grandma Kit said. "But he can't. What on Earth are we going to do with a cat that loves to fish and play in water? Frankie is going to be here for a whole week."

"Grandpa Tom might have some ideas," I said. "Should I wake him up?"

"No," Grandma Kit said. "He finally came to bed about two o'clock this morning. As usual, he played hunting games with the kitties until very late."

"Does he ever play fishing games with them?" I asked.

"I expect so," she said.

"Well, that's what Frankie wants," I said. "I'll have a shower and then look in my cat books. They're full of ideas."

"Good plan," Grandma Kit said.

I headed upstairs, took a quick shower and changed into some clean clothes. Then I got busy reading.

I flipped through one book and then another. And another. And another. Finally I turned a page in my fifth book and stared at the picture I saw there. "That's it," I said.

I tucked the book under my arm and ran back to Tabby Towers.

CHAPTER 8
A purr-fect week

I showed the picture to Grandma Kit.

"That's a great idea," she said. "Frankie would love it. We have the supplies — except the paddling pool. The Wolfes have a few in their doggie play yard. Run over and ask to borrow one. I'm sure Winifred will say yes."

"Can't we just ask Alfreeda?" I said, looking around the room. "Where is she?"

"She had to go home and help for a while," Grandma Kit said. "Winifred called and said they're having trouble with a sheepdog."

The Hound Hotel kennel building was at the end of the Wolfes' long driveway. I rang the doorbell and headed inside. The doorbell sounded like a crazy little dog barking at a mail carrier. *YIP! YIP! YIP!*

"Hello?" I called when the yipping stopped. "It's me, Tabitha."

"Come on back into the corridor, Tabby Cat," Mrs Wolfe said.

I hurried past the front desk and into the corridor. A very big, very dirty sheepdog sat in the middle of the floor. Mrs Wolfe, Alfreeda and her twin brother, Alfie, were pushing on the dog's back. He wasn't moving. At all.

"Come on, Harry. Be good," Alfreeda said. "Everything's going to be okay."

"What's wrong?" I asked.

Mrs Wolfe shook her head. "We can't get this big guy into the grooming room," she said. "He needs a b-a-t-h."

"We can't even say the word out loud, or he cries his head off," Alfie said.

"A dog that doesn't like b-a-t-h-s?" I said, looking right at Alfreeda.

She looked at me, then looked away quickly. I smiled.

"Oh, yeah," Alfie said. "Harry *hates* them. He doesn't even like getting his paws wet."

Alfreeda looked at the ceiling and started to whistle quietly.

"Hmm," I said, still staring at her. "I thought dogs *loved* being in water. I guess all dogs are different. Just like cats."

"Very true," Mrs Wolfe said. She gave Harry another push. He still didn't move.

"Mrs Wolfe, can we borrow one of your paddling pools?" I asked. "It's for Frankie."

"Of course," she said. "Just go out the back and grab one from the yard."

"Awesome. Thank you!" I said. "Good luck with b-a-t-h time!"

❧ ❧ ❧

Back at my grandparents' house, I sprayed the pool with a hose until it looked like new. Then I took it into Tabby Towers and placed it in the middle of the room.

"Is this a good place for Frankie's fishing pond?" I asked Grandma Kit.

"Couldn't be better," she said. "He'll get water on the floor, but that's not a problem. We'll add floor wiping to your list of hotel jobs this week." She smiled at me.

"Fine," I said, smiling back at her. "If it makes Frankie happy, it makes me happy too."

Next, Grandma Kit and I headed to the meadow with a wheelbarrow and two shovels.

We dug up rocks of all sizes. After we cleaned them, we carried them inside. We put the largest rocks around the edge of the "pond".

"Frankie can sit on these rocks and get a good view of the fish," I said. "Let's set up the fountain now."

My parents had given Grandma Kit a garden fountain for her birthday. She hadn't even opened the box yet. I got out the fountain and placed it in the middle of the pool. Grandma Kit read the instructions out loud.

After we got the fountain hooked up, we piled smaller rocks around the base of it. Then we piled the smallest rocks up the sides.

By then, Grandpa Tom had walked in. He yawned, rubbed his eyes and sipped a cup of coffee. I showed him the picture in the book. Suddenly he looked wide-awake.

"An indoor fishing pond for Frankie, our special Bengal?" he said. "Wonderful idea!"

"Can you carve some fish out of wood?" I asked. "I'll paint them."

"Sure," Grandpa Tom said with a grin. "Let's get started."

🐾 🐾 🐾

I stood in Grandpa Tom's workshop, plugging my ears. He was using his super-loud saw to carve fish shapes out of wood.

Better to be plugging my ears than plugging my nose, I thought. *These fish won't stink.*

Grandpa Tom carved fifteen thick wooden fish. "These will float like live fish," he said. "Thinner wood would make them float on their sides, like dead fish. Frankie will be more interested in live prey."

Grandpa Tom and I sanded the edges of the fish so they were smooth. Then we got the quick-dry paint. We chose colours that cats can see best: blue, violet and yellow-green.

I painted the fish in big, colourful patterns. I just knew they'd catch Frankie's eyes – and *he'd* want to catch *them*.

Back in Tabby Towers, Grandpa Tom and I poured buckets of water into the pool. We filled it about three-quarters full.

"The fountain pump will recycle all the water," he said. "I'll plug it in and make sure it's running safely."

Grandpa Tom plugged in the fountain. Water from the pool bubbled out the top. It flowed down the sides, over the rocks and back into the pool. The sound woke Frankie from his nap. He meowed loudly and pawed on his door.

"See what we made for you, boy?" I said, taking him out of his apartment. He leaped out of my arms and landed next to his very own little fishing pond.

I dropped the wooden fish into the pool. The fountain made tiny waves, and the fish bobbed. Frankie fixed his eyes on a blue and violet one.

He stood on a rock, still as stone. He stared at that fish. Slowly, he crept into the water and slid his paw under it. It stopped bobbing, and Frankie slapped it out of the water. It landed on the floor. Frankie jumped over and bit it. Then he leaped back to the pond to hunt for more fish.

He spent the rest of the day fishing. And the rest of the *week* too! Yes, Frankie had a purr-fect week at Tabby Towers, thanks to a bubbling pool filled with wooden fish.

I never wanted to forget how much fun that week was. So it's a good thing I have a photo to help me remember. It was printed in the town newspaper. Alfreeda had taken the picture. She wanted everyone to know about this handsome, water-loving, fun-loving cat.

The coolest thing about the photo is this: Frankie, the Bengal cat, is doing doggy paddle in the paddling pool.

The newspaper had printed these words under the picture: *Can you believe this? It's a DOGGY-paddling cat!*

Of course *I* can believe it. And now, Alfreeda can believe it too.

Is a Bengal the cat for you?

Hello, it's me, Tabitha!

Maybe you'd love to have your own handsome Bengal cat now, right? I'm sure you would. Bengals make great pets for some families.

Here's why: First, Bengal cats are very sweet, friendly, loving, playful and gentle. Second, their beautiful coats are easy to care for. Bengals shed very little. Combing them once a week is enough. Baths aren't needed often.

But before you buy or adopt a Bengal cat, there are some important things you should know:

A Bengal cat comes from crossing a domestic cat with a true wild cat — the Asian leopard. The Bengal cat you choose must be at least "F4". F4 means it is four generations removed from the wild cat. If it isn't, the cat might not act gently enough to live safely with people.

Bengals like company and are VERY active cats. They need a lot of attention and don't like to be left alone. They also need a lot of exercise, and they love to play games. They may even go for walks outside on a lead. Indoors or out, they love to zoom around like racing cars and climb up high. So be sure to give your Bengal a large play space.

Bengals may sometimes suffer from health problems. They may develop problems with their hips, eyes, hearts or kneecaps. It's important that Bengal cat owners plan regular checkups with a vet.

All right, cat lovers! That's all for now . . . until the next adventure at Tabby Towers!

Meowingly yours,

Tabitha Catarina Felinus (Tabby Cat, for short)

Glossary

annoying making someone feel angry or impatient

bait get someone or something to come to you by offering food or another treat

bob bounce up and down, usually in water

collar thin band of leather or other material that a pet wears around its neck

doggy paddle way a dog swims, with chest down and arms or front legs reaching out in front

generation all the members of a group of people or animals born around the same time

instinct behaviour that is natural rather than learned

nocturnal active at night and resting during the day

predator animal that hunts other animals for food

prey animal hunted by another animal for food

vet doctor who cares for animals

Talk about it

1. Explain why losing Frankie could've really hurt Tabby Towers. How would people feel about leaving their cats at the hotel?

2. Look at the illustration on page 33 and describe what's happening in this part of the story.

3. Describe, step by step, how Tabby, Grandma Kit and Grandpa Tom build an indoor fishing pond for Frankie. Begin with Tabby flipping through her cat books, looking for ideas.

Write about it

1. Pretend you're interviewing Frankie for the town newspaper. List three questions and then answer them as if you were Frankie. You might ask about Frankie's love for water, his fishing tips or what he thought of his stay at Tabby Towers.

2. Write a letter to your parents that explains why you think a Bengal would, or would not, be a good cat for your family.

3. Write a one-page essay on Bengal cats. Use at least three sources.

About the author

Shelley Swanson Sateren has been a freelance writer for thirty years and has written more than forty books for children, both fiction and non-fiction. As well as writing, Shelley has worked as a children's book editor and in a children's bookshop. She is also a primary school teacher and has enjoyed employment in several schools. Shelley lives in Minnesota, USA, with her husband and has two grown-up sons.

About the llustrator

Deborah Melmon has worked as an illustrator for more than twenty-five years. After graduating from Academy of Art University in San Francisco, she started her career illustrating covers for the *Palo Alto Weekly* newspaper. Since then, she has produced artwork for more than twenty children's books. Her artwork can also be found on wrapping paper, greeting cards and fabric. Deborah lives in California, USA, and shares her studio with an energetic Airedale Terrier called Mack.

VISIT
TABBY TOWERS
AGAIN WITH
THESE AWESOME
ADVENTURES!

ADVENTURES at TABBY TOWERS
Leaping Lizzie

Queen Lizzie's Pizza Palace

Written by
_____nson Sateren

Illustrated by
Deborah Melmon

ADVENTURES at TABBY TOWERS
Boxing Bootsie

Written by
Shelley Swanson Sateren

Illustrated by
Deborah Melmon

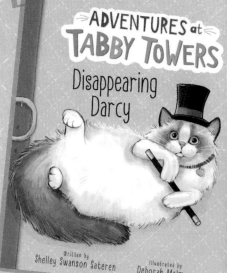

ADVENTURES at TABBY TOWERS
Disappearing Darcy

Written by
Shelley Swanson Sateren

Illustrated by
Deborah Melmon

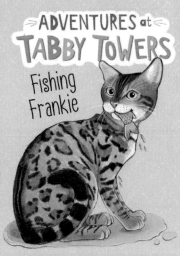

ADVENTURES at TABBY TOWERS
Fishing Frankie

Written by
Shelley Swanson Sateren

Illustrated by
Deborah Melmon

(WE PROMISED ALFREEDA
WE'D INCLUDE THE
HOUND HOTEL GUESTS
AND THEIR SUPER-FUN
STORIES HERE TOO!)

www.raintree.co.uk